# The First Dive

by Rose Howell
illustrated by Gary Undercuffler

BEST PRACTICES IN READING
Classroom Library

# Chapter One

Alex put his bathing suit into his suitcase. He was both nervous and excited.

"Boy, are you lucky," said his best friend, Matt. "I wish I had a cousin in Florida. You'll have warm weather, sand, and sun."

Alex knew he was lucky. It would be a nice break from the busy city. It wasn't just the sand and sun that he was excited about. He knew that he was going to go diving. About ten years ago, his cousin Michael started a scuba diving shop and school on the Florida coast. People could rent diving equipment and learn how to dive there. Alex had been wanting to dive since he was eight years old. But he had to wait until he was older to take lessons.

Michael told him that after a few lessons he'd be diving in the ocean. Alex thought to himself, "Will it be like those TV shows? Maybe I'll make friends with a dolphin or find hidden treasure!"

On the way to Florida, Alex imagined all the exciting things he would be able to tell Matt about when he got back. Alex was still thinking about hidden treasure when Carly knocked on the door. He didn't even hear her.

"Alex, open up. It's me!" she finally shouted.

Carly was all ready to go. "I can't wait to go diving," she said. "Scuba diving is like floating in the clouds."

His sister had talked about scuba diving for years. Alex had always wanted to try it.

"I'm trying to hurry," he said. "I want to get there early enough to dive today."

Carly laughed. "It's not that simple," she said. "You have to learn about scuba diving before you can do it. First you will have to take a class."

The next day, they left Michael's house and walked downstairs to the diving shop. Carly walked Alex to the class. He tried not to show how nervous he was.

"I'll meet you here for your lunch break," Carly said. "This envelope has your medical forms in it. Oh, and here's a notebook and some pencils."

Alex didn't think he needed a notebook. But before he could say anything, Carly had left. Alex went in and looked around. He was in a room with desks, a chalkboard, and seven other people. Maybe there was some mistake. He wanted to learn how to scuba dive. He was sure you needed to learn in the water. He looked around for his cousin. Alex wondered if Michael had played a trick on him. Just then a man walked into the room. It was the scuba diving teacher.

"Please sit down," he said. "We have a lot to do. Every minute counts."

Alex found a seat and looked at the other students. They were all different ages.

"I'm Dave," the teacher said. "Welcome to the start of a great adventure. Diving is fun, but it has rules. You have to learn those rules well. The ocean can be a dangerous place."

Dave walked over to a table full of equipment.

"Everything on this table is important to a diver. It's all diving gear. When you use these things correctly, you will discover the amazing world beneath the sea. However, if you don't learn to use it the right way, you will have nothing but trouble."

Dave asked the students to introduce themselves and say a few words. One couple wanted to try something they'd never done before. Another couple was retired. They were looking for a new hobby. A girl named Krista hoped to become a veterinarian. She wanted to learn about life underwater. Alex said he had wanted to dive ever since his sister had learned how.

"So, when do we go on our first dive?" someone asked. Dave said that they had a lot to learn before they could go underwater in the ocean.

"Every morning we will have class for about two hours. Then we'll break for lunch. In the afternoon, we'll meet at the pool and work there. There will be a quiz every day to test what you've learned."

Then he handed out the textbooks.

Alex thought for sure he was in the wrong place. He didn't need to be an expert. He just wanted to dive. His cousin had never said anything about going to summer school! Alex raised his hand.

"I think I might be in the wrong class," he said. "I don't need to do fancy stuff. I just want to swim underwater."

Someone laughed, but Dave just smiled.

"No one can scuba dive without taking a class like this. Diving underwater means learning to breathe and move in a different world. There is no air underwater. We are not fish. We don't have gills or fins. So we have to learn to use this gear and our brains. Underwater, this is your best friend." Dave held up an air tank.

Alex looked at the tank and thought about Matt, his real best friend. Matt was probably out playing basketball. Would Matt still think that Alex was lucky?

"This tank lets you breathe underwater," said Dave. "It is filled with about as much air as this room is."

He opened the door to the room behind him. "That's more than enough air to get you down into the ocean and back up. You'll have lots of time to enjoy the wonderful world underwater. I am going to pair each of you with a buddy. You and your buddy will be a team. Everyone has to have a buddy to dive."

"Krista and Alex, you will be buddies," Dave added.

Alex was happy. Krista was closest to his age.

"Hi, Alex," said Krista. She reached out to shake his hand.

"Hi," said Alex.

Carly was waiting at the door when the class let out for lunch.

"Well, what do you think so far?" she asked.

"I didn't know it would be so much work," Alex said. "I thought we'd get right into the water and start learning. Dave gave us a textbook. We'll have quizzes every day. It's like school. You're so lucky! You can sit on the beach and relax."

"I took a course like this four years ago. I remember thinking there's so much to learn, too," said Carly.

"That's just what I was thinking," said Alex.

"Well, Alex, as Grandpa used to say . . . 'Nothing worth doing is easy.' Look at the underwater pictures in your textbook. Wouldn't you like to see all that for yourself?"

"I guess so," Alex answered. But he didn't sound so sure.

"You'll feel better when you get into the water," said Carly.

 What made Alex interested in scuba diving?

 How does Alex feel about the class?

 What does Carly tell Alex to make him feel more hopeful about learning how to dive? Do you think she is right?

 Why do you think a diver would need to take classes before diving?

# Chapter Two

Later that day, the class met back at the pool.

"First things first," said Dave, "I want to be sure that you are all comfortable in the water. So I'm going to test you, two at a time. Everyone stand with your buddy. You'll get in the water together. You will need to swim 200 yards. Then you'll have to float or tread water for ten minutes. I'll time you."

Alex watched the buddies go into the pool. Then it was his turn. Alex and Krista started swimming. After several laps, Alex floated on his back. "This is much better than being in the classroom," he thought. He was a pretty good swimmer. But he still wasn't diving. What if he failed the quizzes? Would he still get to dive?

Alex planned to find Carly as soon as the class ended. But he realized that he couldn't rely on her to make everything right. He had to sort it out by himself!

On the second day, the class learned more about the diving gear. Dave held up a mask.

"You wear a mask so you can see underwater," Dave said as he put it on.

"This is very important for a safe and enjoyable dive. Go to the diving shop and try on masks. Spend time making sure that your mask fits you just right. The woman in the shop will help you. You will need to be able to squeeze your nose. You can borrow a mask from the shop for tomorrow's class."

Then Dave held up a pair of fins.

"Fins will help you move like a fish in the water," he said. "The soft shoes that keep your feet warm inside the fins are called booties. Please bring fins and booties to the next class."

Then Dave showed them a belt with dials on it. "This is a gauge belt. It has a compass, a pressure gauge, and a depth gauge. The pressure gauge tells you when the air is running out and it's time to go back up to the surface. The depth gauge and compass tell you where you are."

"Isn't this exciting?" asked Krista.

"It's a lot to learn," answered Alex.

At the pool, Dave showed them some more gear. He was dressed in a slippery-looking suit.

"A wet suit will keep you warm. You'll need one for our ocean dives. You can get one in the dive shop. It won't cost you anything since you are taking this class."

Dave showed them a vest with a lot of pockets.

"This is your BCD. That stands for Buoyancy Control Device. You need this to carry your air tank. It will help keep you buoyant underwater. That means that you won't sink down or float up. You inflate the vest with air. But you'll need more than that." He picked up some silver-colored blocks.

"These are weights. They go in this weight belt. This will also help keep you at the perfect weight underwater."

Then Dave showed the class how to wear the mouthpiece and diving mask. The class was quiet as Dave put in his mouthpiece and went into the pool. Soon he was gliding along in the water.

"I can't wait," said Krista.

"I can," said another woman.

Alex said nothing. He hoped that no one would notice that his knees were shaking. "Breathing underwater is easy for Dave," thought Alex. "But Dave's been using scuba equipment for years. What will happen when I have to get into the pool wearing all that equipment? What if I forget how to use the mouthpiece?"

After class, Alex met up with Carly. They went to their cousin's shop. It was full of all the gear that Dave had shown them. There were masks and fins and booties. There were those special vests. "What did Dave called them?" Alex wondered. The sign said BCDs. Alex tried to remember what that stood for. Buoyancy Control Devices, that was it!

The woman in the store knew just what Alex needed. His sister knew, too. Alex tried on wet suits, masks, BCD vests, fins, and weight belts.

They walked back to their cousin's house and went to Carly's room. She opened a small suitcase and showed Alex her diving gear.

"Go try yours on and then I'll help you with the gear," she said.

Soon Alex was standing in his wet suit and his vest.

"Look at me in a BCD," said Alex.

Carly laughed and helped him with the mask, the fins, and the mouthpiece. She hung the gauge belt on his BCD. Then came the weight belt and weights.

Alex looked in the mirror.

"I look like an alien," he laughed.

"My little brother looks like a real diver!" said Carly.

The next day, the class practiced putting on their gear.

"This afternoon we will put on all our gear and go into the pool,"said Dave. "Before we do that, we will need to go over a few more things."

Dave talked about how water pressure could hurt their ears.

"To prevent ear pain, you must release ear pressure as you go down into the water. To do that, you squeeze your nose. You have to do this many times as you go down."

Then he showed them how to read the gauges on their belts. He handed out sheets of paper with the hand signals they would need underwater.

Alex practiced the hand signals with Krista. In just a few hours, that would be their only way of talking to each other.

**UNDERSTANDING FICTION**

1. What are some of the things Alex has learned in the class?

2. Why do divers need to use hand signals?

3. What would diving be like without all the gear?

4. How do you think Alex feels about diving now?

# Chapter Three

That afternoon, the class met at the pool. They put on their gear. Dave checked to see that everyone was ready. He told them to remember to squeeze their noses as they went down into the water. Then Dave went over some hand signals to make sure that everyone understood them.

"Remember, try to be like a fish. Don't move around wildly. Move slowly and gently. Keep an eye on your buddy at all times. Relax and take a deep breath. Remember not to hold your breath, just breathe normally. Now let's get in the water."

Alex wasn't sure he could relax. At that moment, he wished Michael had owned a bookstore instead of a diving school! Suddenly, Dave gave a signal and splash! They all went into the water.

Alex made sure that he could see Krista. He made sure he could see Dave, too. They moved through the water. Alex was surprised at how light he felt. Out of the water, the gear had been heavy, but underwater it was light.

Dave made the sign for "Okay" to the class. They all gave him an "Okay" sign back. Then they swam around the pool. It didn't really feel like ordinary swimming, thought Alex. It felt more like gliding.

Dave had the class pretend that their masks were flooded with water. He showed them how to clear them. He made them check their gauges. When he gave the hand signal to go up to the surface, the whole class went up together slowly.

"Good job!" said Dave, as they took off their gear. "See you all in class tomorrow morning."

The next day in class, Dave started right away.

"Today we'll talk about fear," he said. He made a list on the chalkboard. "Sharks" was first on the list.

Dave explained that sharks were not a real danger. There were other things in the water that were much more dangerous.

"I heard box jellyfish can kill you in minutes," said one man.

"This is true," Dave said. "But box jellyfish live around Australia, not Florida. No one would let you dive if they were around."

Dave also talked about the fear of running out of air. He said there was more than enough air in the tank and they would practice breathing over and over again.

Finally, it was the day of their first ocean dive. In the morning, everyone met in the classroom. Dave gave them some last-minute instructions.

"Remember, try to be like a fish. Keep your arms at your sides. Don't hold your breath. Squeeze your nose many times while going down. Clear your mask if it gets flooded." Then he showed them again how to do that.

"Where do we keep rocks and shells that we want to take back as souvenirs?" someone asked.

"That's a good question," said Dave. "We take nothing back with us, and the only things we leave behind are bubbles. The only things we take are photos. You can't bring a camera with you until the course is finished. So, right now, all you can bring back are memories."

After the class was over, Alex went to meet Carly. On his way, he saw a woman crying in pain. She was wearing a wet suit and walking into the dive shop. People were gathered around her. A doctor pushed his way through the crowd.

"What happened?" asked Alex.

"Ear trouble," someone said, "she popped her ear drum."

Alex found Carly. "Did you see that woman crying?" he asked. "I don't know if I'm ready to do this. Maybe this is a sign."

Carly put her arm around him. "I wouldn't let you dive if I thought it was too dangerous. Mom and Dad wouldn't have let me bring you here, and Cousin Michael said you were ready. Dave says you're a good student. I heard that the woman forgot to squeeze her nose on the way down."

"But is it worth it?" asked Alex. "There's all this gear and so much danger!"

"You've worked so hard," said Carly. "It's a chance to see a whole new, beautiful world. Your fear will make you careful."

At the last minute, one of the men in Alex's class backed out. Maybe he had seen the woman crying. Alex wasn't sure which was smarter—backing out or diving. Maybe he would feel better if he quit, too.

Carly kept telling him that he could do it. She showed him photos from her dives. "Remember, nothing worth doing is easy," she reminded him.

He heard Carly's voice in his head as he stood on the boat. He and his classmates put on their gear. Krista gave him a hug. Dave made sure they were ready.

Splash! Alex watched as his classmates stepped onto the platform. Then they took a giant stride into the ocean. He could feel his heart pounding.

Suddenly, Alex was in the water. He squeezed his nose and went down, down, down.

Alex kept his eyes on Krista and on Dave. He was diving! He was underwater! Dave gave him an "Okay" hand signal. So did Krista. Alex gave one back.

They glided among the fish. It was like being inside one of Carly's photos. Plants on and around the coral reef swayed gently. Alex remembered to keep his hands by his sides. He moved his fins gently. He felt like a fish. There was so much to see! It was so quiet that the only noise he heard was the hiss of the bubbles from his tank.

He didn't know the names of all the fish he saw. But he did recognize the angel fish. Dave pointed out different things for the class to look at, including some fish that were motionless. Then Dave signaled for everyone to go up. They went up slowly. Dave signaled for them to check their gauges and pause at 15 feet. Then they were to go to the surface and into the boat.

Alex couldn't believe it! They were back on the boat. He had done it! Everyone hugged and talked about what they saw.

"Remember when I pointed to those motionless fish?" Dave asked.

"Well, those were nurse sharks."

"Sharks! Wait until I tell Matt," Alex thought.

Then they all described what they had seen on the dive. They looked everything up in the books on the boat.

"There will be four more dives in our course," said Dave. "After that, you take a written test to become certified divers."

Alex went on the other dives with his class, and he passed the written test. To celebrate passing the course, Carly, Krista, and Alex all went out for ice cream.

After Alex was certified, he was ready for the best dive of all. This time, Carly was Alex's buddy. She checked and rechecked his gear.

"Remember not to touch anything that is too beautiful or too ugly," Carly told him. "That's what is most likely to be poisonous."

"I know," said Alex. "Besides, Dave taught us to keep our hands to ourselves."

Carly tested him on hand signals.

"Don't worry so much," said Alex. "Remember, you're the one who convinced me I could do it."

"You're right," she said. "Let's go!"

Soon they were both in the ocean. Carly snapped Alex's picture underwater.

"I hope Mom and Dad will let me make this into a giant poster," he thought.

When they got home, Alex looked at some of the postcards he'd bought. They showed many of the fish that he had seen underwater. He was trying to decide which ones to keep and which ones to give Matt.

"I still can't believe I did it!" he said. "These pictures don't even show how amazing it really was!"

Carly laughed. "I hate to say I told you so, but I did!"

"Can we do this again soon?" Alex asked. "Maybe you'll let me use the camera next time. Maybe we can go on a night dive. I heard it's fun to explore underwater wrecks. Maybe Matt can join us next time!"

"Oh, no! No more beginner's nerves for me!" said Carly. "We'll do this again, but not right away. No night dives or wrecks just yet. Let's take it one step at a time."

"I think you mean one splash at a time," said Alex.